Ten Little Dogs

WRITTEN AND ILLUSTRATED BY

RUTH BROWN

Scallywag Press Ltd

LONDON

10

Ten little dogs
sitting in a line –

One chased a butterfly,
and then there were . . .

9

Nine little dogs
    peeping through a gate –

One crawled underneath,
and then there were . . .

8

Eight little dogs
snacking at eleven –

One stole an empty bowl,
and then there were . . .

Seven little dogs
having fun with sticks –

One got stuck between the trees,
and then there were . . .

6 **Six** little dogs creeping round a hive –

One was chased by bees,
and then there were . . .

5

Five little dogs
having a tug of war –

One got soaking wet,
and then there were . . .

4

Four little dogs
  paddling in the sea –

One had his tail nipped,
and then there were . . .

3

Three little dogs
   playing 'Peek-a-boo' –

One found a hiding place,
and then there were . . .

Two little dogs
dozing in the sun –

One heard his playmates,
and then there was . . .

1

One little dog
all alone, but then –

he ran to find the others,
and then there were . . .

10

Ten little dogs
   romping in the park!

Oh, what a noise they made –

Bark!